Pathw

GW01034065

The Anthology

Edited By Alkimu

Contents

Main Partners	Manchester City Council & LIME
Researchers	Carolyn Kagan & Judith Sixsmith – MMU
Management	Brian Chapman, Lime
Advisory Group	Langley Brown, Arts and Mental Health Consultant; Sally Carr, Manchester City Council Joint Health Unit; Brian Chapman, Director Lime; Dr Ceri Dornan, Mental Health Lead GP South Manchester Primary Care Trust; David Haley, Manchester Institute for Research and Innovation in Art and Design [MIRIAD] at MMU; Wendy Henry, Coordinator South Manchester Healthy Living Network; John Lucy, Director of Public Health South Manchester Primary Care Trust; Richard Michael Art & Regeneration Manager, Manchester City Council

Central Manchester Pathways:

Lead Artists	ALKIMU – Muli Amaye and Kim Wiltshire
Supporting Artists	Toni Bysouth, Yasmin Yaqub
Volunteers	Cheryl Marney, Melanie Macdonald
Venues	YASP, African Womens Art Development, Claremont Resource Centre, The Foyer, The Powerhouse

South Manchester Pathways:

| Lead Artist | Irene Lumley |
| Supporting Artists | Adela Jones, Talia Theatre, Jessica Bockler, Tina Foran, Andrew Rowlands, Gemma Parker, Matt Vale, Rob Vale |

| **Venues** | Family Action Benchill, Newall Green High School for the Arts, Studio One, Tree of Life Centre, Nathan Road Lone Parents Project, Hall Lane Resource Centre Day Hospital |

All work included in this anthology was completed during Pathways workshop sessions. Permission has been sought where possible for the works included in this anthology and authors retain copyright of their own work.

Please note that some of the works contain swear words, which some people may find offensive, and should not be read by children under under 14 years of age.

ISBN:0-9543362-4-0   © Alkimu/Lime Pathways

Introduction

What is Pathways?

Pathways is a programme of creative activity around mental health and well being in the community. The project was piloted in Wythenshawe and lead by artist Irene Lumley. The second phase, central Manchester, started one year later and was lead by writing partnership ALKIMU, whilst the pilot project continued to work with small groups in Wythenshawe. Artists worked with local people to find ways of overcoming emotional difficulties and the daily stresses associated with ill health to ensure general well-being.

ALKIMU, writers Muli Amaye and Kim Wiltshire, worked over a period of six months with small groups of local people in Longsight, Levenshulme, Hulme and Moss Side. The groups were informal and set up to explore new ideas through non-threatening creative activity – no artistic skills required! What follows here is a selection of prose, poetry and photograghy from the creative writing and visual art workshops from the Central Manchester Pathways Project.

Poems entitled 'The Box' came from a writing exercise used by ALKIMU, but as the results were so diverse and interesting it was decided to include them in the Anthology. All the work is the participants' own, except for pieces that are 'Edited by Alkimu', as these have come from oral stories and have been re-created as poetry. For many participants, this is the first time they have had their creative work published, and so we hope you enjoy the first Pathways Anthology.

ALKIMU
February 2005

Pathways Mission Statement

"To explore avenues of creativity within the community and show how the arts through creative activity can play an important role in the mitigating against mental ill health."

Ten years Ago...

I was twelve years old
Living in Hulme wagging school
Seeing flats getting knocked down
Pink ones yellow ones
      All around

Playing truant with my sister, getting up to
      All kinds
A good girl was hard to find
Wanting to do what gangs
Were doing
      Collecting bottles
Petrol would fill em
Thrown   bang bang
      Killin
Population 10 million

Negative thoughts for such
A young age, no wonder
      The world is filled with such rage!

But where did it
Start who do they blame
They blame us from the
Ghettos's bul all
      That is
Is their war budget

We commit crime, they
      Get pay rise
To go 2 war
N control mankind!

Leanne Brown

Wooden Spoon Diva

There is the house, the cat
And me
And everything that symbolises
My creativity
Needlecraft, drawing and my
Writing poetry
Playing music has been put to
Rest, has been replaced by my
Singing

There I'll be in the kitchen, with
The utensils forever ringing
With the cat chiming in, with the
Occasional 'meow'
With the infrequent parties, people
Getting drunk falling down
With an 'ow!'

Then I'll be clubbing it, by
The end of the night my head
Will be swimming
But I'd be still on the dance
Floor shimmying

The occasional visit to the cinema
Will be to see a sci-fi or a horror
I have always loved walking
Which is just as well, with my attempts
At cycling.

Naomi Wilson

The Box [1]

The box
What everyone sees
From soaps to reality
This is what we call TV
To me it's called
Telly LIE Vision

Full of lies
Full of wrong decisions
The thing that attracts us is all the bright colours
Celebrity bargain deals
It helps poor people want to steal
It puts single mums under pressure
For the latest games, trainers, new coat whatever the weather
It's full of violence, political debates
But we all watch this, all of our mates!

This is what this box can do
Make millions from me and you

Whatever we see, we choose to believe
And we all have to pay, for a licence to watch it every day

It's mad when you think what this box can do
Sit us down and keep us tuned
Make us spend
Make us watch it to the end
Make us laugh
Make us cry
That's the box
That relates to me

Leanne Brown

My Wife

Wife, wife it is morning
Wife, wife can I have breakfast
Wife, wife the baby is crying
Wife, wife I have finished my breakfast
Wife, wife the baby needs cleaning
Wife, wife can I have a cuppa
Wife, wife the baby needs feeding
Wife, wife what can I do without you?

Ehi Oboh

When I was twenty

When I was twenty I was married
Not of my own free will
In the Caribbean it was arranged you see
So at twenty I was married
For forty six years

We came over and I trained
To be a nurse
And now I am retired
We are from Ghiana and
My husband decided we are
Going back home

In 2001 he came back for an
Operation it was not successful
I went back home
But my children are here
There is nothing out there for me
No family when I go back home

They come and visit but they are
All working here
Ten hours on a flight
Too much even for sunshine
So I'm coming back home

Mrs Bond
Edited by Alkimu

Chair : Naomi Wilson

Ten years ago

Ten years ago I was young
Ten years now I'm old
Ten years ago was marriage
Ten years now I'm separated
Ten years ago I was in an old job
Ten years now I am in a new job
Now and then still with lovely children
That, nothing can buy

Augustina O Agbaje

The Box [2]

The box is my living room
I like it because it is a place where I can relax
I can watch TV in
Sometimes I eat inside
I can do anything in my living room

Could you imagine how it is so well to stay
In the living room?
You have all you need
On your left
On your right
In front of you
Behind you
There is good music
And a TV with lots of programmes

Treasur Mwatiba

The House

Crunching down the long gravel path, I look up towards the towering house. The image of it is burned on my memory, like a hellish fingerprint every time I close my eyes. My heart in my mouth, I reach forward and knock cautiously on the cold wooden door; the sound echoing eerily inside the otherwise silent house. A million questions shoot through my mind – why am I here? Why did I come here? Jumping back at the slow painful creak as the door gives way under my tentative knock, I struggle to adjust my eyes to the dim light. Taking in my surroundings, I make the split second decision to allow myself to be swallowed by this monster of a house.

Sophie Davies

Where I Live

The place where I live is rubbish
The people there are shit
I don't feel safe
Nowhere I go

It makes me feel like
My world's gonna end
The only thing that keeps me going
Is the baby
And my girlfriend

I'm looking forward to a better future

William

Five pound a week

I'm one that did come into this country
A long time ago
Almost seventy years
In those days it was terrible cos
I come straight from the boat to the Hospital
At Withington, that is the first place I worked
I was a nurse and in the midst of those days
We didn't know any lift or anything
We had to lift them up with our own strength
And my wages was five pound a week

Bed pan we had to wash ourselves in a big
Concrete place, we have to wash them with a brush
And my wages was five pound a week

I was so scared cos we have to sign the paper
That if we drop the patient we will be in trouble
I said to myself I just come from Jamaica
I don't know nothing about trouble and if I get
Into trouble what will happen to me
The other nurse did let go and walk away
The patient did fall on me and they had to come and
Lift her. Three nurses it took
And my stomach was up and out and did rupture
They had to perform operation and until today I
Never able to come on my feet
And my wages was five pound a week

But God help me and take control
That I able to survive and live till I am 84

Young people must remember
True love will overcome everything

Ask God to give uno peace
Whatever you do God will bless you

Mrs Griffiths
Edited by Alkimu

Ushauri Kuhusu Kuandika Story

Africa wannsikia kuwa Englan ni rahisi kufanya kila kitu unatum. Electric kama unataka kwend mahdi hubali unatumia njia ya ralis na mangi wanasikia. Na nilipo ika hapa naona tofauti pai ukisonia story book utaona story inasema kuilinisu Africa wana fill. Sad kwa lujo mimi na shauri nivizuri kuandika truu story and furaha stor kaia kila upande.

Saynab

The Box [3]

An ornamental box could hold
Your jewellery or your money

A toy box filled with childish things
To them would be rather funny
Boxes crammed with books and clothes
To help you move your stuff
A huge box to hide away in
When things get pretty rough

Sophie Davies

Positive/Negative

I was a proud mother
It was great
I was in Badagy
It was not bad
I was independent
It was fun
I was prayerful
It was good
I was a community champion
It was a challenge
I was a school head
It was the best

Sad happiness turn sadness
Sad life is not fair
Sad to be relocating
Sad to miss my old friends
Sad I have to start again
Sad I did not listen
Sad I did not look out
Sad that dreams are just dreams
Sad
But open to happiness and love

Ehi Oboh

The Queen and my evening dress

I went down to Buckingham Palace
Myself and my son.
It's such a long time ago now,
I can't even remember what the Queen said
When she gave Andrew his award and
I went down to Buckingham Palace

I went down to Buckingham Palace
And me dress was an evening dress
Nice evening dress, could have been velvet
Could have been blue, or black
It's a long time ago now, when
I went down to Buckingham Palace

I went down to Buckingham Palace
In me nice, velvet evening dress
And when the Queen saw me she was shocked
By my beautiful velvet evening dress
But I can't remember what she said to me
It was so long ago that
I went down to Buckingham Palace

From stories by Auntie Hazel
Edited by Alkimu

Wonderland

I think and think, until I
Wink and blink that I need
A pink drink from the sink

On emerging from the sink
I discover that I am
Beginning to shrink and
Start to believe that I
Am Alice, in Wonderland

Whilst dangling over the
Edge of the sink, I start
To become aware of my
Size. Finally I am sitting
On the worktop and discover
That I'm only fifty inches
High

I think and think, now
The world is my oyster

I look at my sink and
Start to think, I believe could
I have a bath or shower
And also have a swim in
Here

While I'm thinking such things
I think I'll just jump in and
Have a quick shower under the
Tap before I start to stink

Also, I believe that if I
Don't stop thinking I might
Just disappear and go POP!

I just can't help myself, it's
The way things go; hop, skip
And think. There I go again
Shrink and shrink, now I'm
Twenty inches tall.

I wonder if there is anything
In this wonderland of mine
That will get me back to my
Normal size. I look at the
Tap, I think 'You sap, I bet
The answer is in there,'

As I reach for the tap
I fall into the sink
When I thought I'd had
My last thought, someone
Comes in and turns on
The tap.

There I am, going round
And round the sink with
Screams of joy and laughing with glee.

Thinking life's a big adventure
When all of a sudden, I feel
Myself go flying through the air.
I land on the ground with a
Great thud on my bum.

Then I hear a voice echoing around
Me and it is laughing hysterically
I look around to see where the
Voice is coming from.

In front of me, is a Persian cat of
The white variety.
She lifts her right paw to scold
Me, she opens her mouth and says,
'What have I told you about
Playing with water?'
I don't understand, it's not as
Though I'm her daughter.

Then I feel myself being lifted
Into the air.
When I'm finally on the ground
I'm fixed in a stare.
Straight ahead of me is a mirror,
Maybe, what I see is an error.

Naomi Wilson

A Picture of Life

Dream
You need to dream for a dream to come true

As a child
I dreamt of palaces, fairytales, beauty and riches.

As a teenager
I dreamt of exams, success and riches.

As a woman
I dreamt of marriage and motherhood.

Today
I dream of my goals
I focus on my target

My dream is priceless

Ehi Oboh

The Sky

I am in the sky now
I feel peace and silence
Here everything is blue and white
I can watch the people in the street and they can't feel my
Presence or see me

This is magic
Because I can fly and...
Oh
This is just a dream
I wish to never wake up again and continue my
Lovely dream

Lucia Castro

Drinking Part 1

I'm a drinker
I wish I was not
If I stopped I could tie the knot
Why can't I stop?
Because I'm a mop

Everyone tells me I should stop
That's what I'm going to do
Not stop completely
Just cut down
'Do you want a drink Rob?'
'Aye, go on, get us a pint then.'

One pint turns into more with you
You're such a screw when you throw
That pint down your neck
'Get us another whisky'
I won't get frisky
On your next whisky

Robert Sutton

"Me, 10 years ago"

Making changes,
A positive transition of physical
A positive transition of mental
The slow realisation,
Drugs don't mix with my chemistry,
The slow realisation,
Social circles must change,
I will do it,
I can do it,
Urges still exist,
But soon forgotten
Slowly people become a thing of the past,
Places become distant memories,
Other social settings are found,
And new people become good friends
Self control, self esteem, self image

Cheryl Marney

A Prayer

Lord help me live from day to day
In search of self, forgetful ways
That even when I knelt down to pray
My prayer shall be for others

Help me in all the things I do
To ever be sincere and true
And know that all I do for thee
Must need be done for others

And when my life on earth is done
And my new life in heaven's begun
May I forget the crown I've won
By still thinking of others

Aunty Grace
Edited by Alkimu

The Box [4]

This is a box
It is yellow
My mother like this box
We use this box for keeping food.
When I am hungry, I open the box to get the peanuts.

I wonder if my neighbour has one.

Daniel Yupet

Paradise

I can see lots of flowers, all different colours, meadows full. It's very euphoric and relaxing, like a very safe place away from earth. The moon is out and all the stars are twinkling - are we all being watched by those in heaven?

I get this strange feeling, then all of a sudden this tree appears. It's different from any other tree - very big, with stars pouring out of its trunk. It's brilliant. I wonder if it's the tree of life?

Wandering around the meadows of flowers, I look up and see plenty of clouds, but one of them is different from all the rest - it has a gold look to it. I take one step on - and off I go into the starry eyed sky, then I am placed on the moon. I can smell something strange - like cheese. Of course! The moon is made of cheese. I can see everything from up here, but I get this strange feeling. Then I see this little girl crying, "Little girl, why are you crying?" I ask. She looks at me and replies, "I need to go back to heaven." "You need to step onto this gold cloud and you will get there - you can trust it, it's a magic cloud," I tell her. So she took one step on to the cloud, it split into two and off she went, down the starry blue sky, and when I followed down the sky, we both flew back to heaven.

Then, there is a reflection of me in a lake ... I look brilliant, my body is brand new, with no scars, I feel surprised but very happy that they've gone. I don't know where the little girl has gone, all I know is that I'm in a wonderful place, very relaxing and stress-free and I realise that the little girl has gone off to her spirit and I will never see her again.

My jeans have twinkling moons on, and my t-shirt has stars all over, and my coat is made of moon rock and looks stunning – but my shoes! They are really fast, I can fly with them on. They have stars on, little jets, they are brilliant.

I start to fly, and see an ounce of skunk on the floor with a diamond ring. I fly down, put the ring on, and the weed turns to a bag of ash, and there is a strange piece of paper, with writing on. It says 'Death Pass' – I feel confused and scared. All of a sudden, a fog comes towards me. Something steps out of the fog – I can see horns and a tail, a fork with a ring of fire round it – I scream "It's the devil!" – then the worry and paranoia come on. He seems angry, annoyed, I can see 666 written on his head, and he has an evil look as he tells me, "I am Lucifer and I've come to take your soul back to hell with me." "No you're not, go away, go away, you can't take me, go back to hell!" I scream, as he throws bolts of fire that burn me. A voice cries "Leave that boy alone, Lucifer, he's mine."

The sky cracks open and I see Jesus, lifting me back to heaven.

There you go. I experienced my final time – am I dreaming, am I not? Who will ever know?

Robert Sutton

I was walking

I was walking in a place, a place that I never saw before
It was cold and hot
I felt so strange
Because it was silent and when I walked I could feel my
Footsteps were soft
And my skin was pale

The place is white and smells of flowers
I feel sad
I feel happy
I want to cry but I want to laugh too

I feel a hand touching my shoulder
And a soft voice whispers softly into my ear
'Welcome to Paradise'

Leandra

The Baptism

When I was a small child
I did go to church regularly
I loved going to church
But I wasn't baptised

When I was nineteen
I went to the pastor
Pastor, I say, I love the Lord
I want to be baptised

Son, the pastor say to me
You are very young at nineteen
With a lot of living yet to do
You can't be baptised

Now I am an old man
I live in England and up to today
I have one regret in my life
I am still not baptised

Mr Ferguson
Edited by Alkimu

Drinking : Robert Sutton

Trapped

When I feel like killing myself
I feel trapped because the people
I love the most
Will hate me if I succeed

But I feel trapped with depression
All the pills can help in the short term
But cannot help in the long run

I feel alcohol is more like a getaway
And not a social drug
People say why do you cut yourself?
Because it helps me feel better
It's pleasure pain
It sounds weird
But it's mine

Robert Sutton

My Journey

Every journey requires a step
So my father says
A step of faith or that of doubt
Some have lifted me up while some made me go round
And round
Like a ring without end
But how could I have walked if I didn't know how to fall
And crawl, I wonder

Remembering boarding school...
Oh my home, oh my home
When shall I see my home
Oh that the days could be shortened
That I might be with my family again
Away from the bullies
No more sleepless nights
No more tears

Clock is ticking
Final exam being written
Agony of waiting for results
Yet another bridge to cross
Never mind...

No more being bullied
No more hiding from those seniors
No more sleepless nights
And no more tears

Home here I come...

Olayinka Arowosegbe

Student Life

School time has come
Switch off the TV
Pack up your toys
And go to bed

Student life
Waking at six a.m.
Prepare for classes
Without breakfast
Student life
Walk in a cold
Dark morning in winter

Student life
Meals are beans and toast every day
Sometimes one has to starve to save
For a night club
Student life
It's funny, but needs hard work
For a better future

Daniel Yupet

Baby's Life

This is how you make me feel:

Great
Happy
Proud
A new life ahead

You are someone to fight for
To live for and protect
You bring light into my life
Cherish, joy, fun and
Love

William

Going to Bed

She screams
She shouts
She pulls my hair
She runs up and down
Almost any where

She laughs
She cries
She jumps on the chairs

I shout
I play
I put her to bed
When she's asleep
I rest my head

Joanne Burnham

School, school

My daughter at three and a half
Walked boldly in and stayed until
Now. One morning for school, school
My daughter cried mummy mummy
My leg is hurting so I bought
A car

It was my job as mummy mummy
To bring my daughter up right
Have you had a wash? Have you
Cleaned your teeth? Are you Dressed?

My daughter went to university
Mummy, mummy you must go too
I didn't want to go, I couldn't do the
Lesson but she came for me and
Took me in her Car

She told the teacher to make sure
That mummy didn't leave the room
And I stayed and I learned and I
Left university. My daughter was so
Proud

And then came my stroke and I was
No longer mummy mummy
My daughter asks me daily, mummy
Have you had a wash? Mummy have
You cleaned your teeth?
Are you dressed?

Mrs Bell
Edited by Alkimu

The Box [5]

The box is my TV
I watch it all day long
I watch comedy, romance, action, horror and cartoons

I enjoy the box [films and soap operas]
Sometimes it makes me laugh
Sometimes it makes me cry
The TV is my friend
And I would miss not having it there

Taneshia Grant

One-way ticket to Fairyland

I am lying on the ground with my eyes closed, listening to everything around me. Opening my eyes, I find myself looking towards the sky. I see what looks like a giant mushroom over-shadowing me. It is brightly coloured. The stem and the inside are dark blue. I get up and walk away, I look back at the mushroom – the top is blue with orange spots.

I look around and notice that there is a thin mist slowly fading away. I shiver in the cold morning air. This place makes me feel as though I have just climbed into a dream. Just when I am thinking that it is so quiet, I hear what sounds like bells. Not the clanging type; it's more like a distant tinkling.

Then a smell eases its way through the coldness of the air and up my nose. The sweet scent of flowers lingering nearby. I notice the smell first because I haven't realised how close the flowers are until I walk on a bit. Right by me, there are a number of thick green stems. I walk by one, and trip over what looks like a long thin leaf protruding from the stem. I look up and see several giant flower heads. I am standing here, thinking, oh goodness, where am I?

Walking and looking around, I notice something very odd. Standing near a lake is a vacuum cleaner. I walk over to it, kneel down and lean over the water. As I reach for the water, I catch the reflection of my face in the lake. I look tired and overcome. I splash my face with some water and swallow some at the same time and get up.

As I get up, I notice something about my feet – they have changed. My shoes have disappeared and my feet have leathery soles. This really feels weird. Whilst looking up and feeling a bit disorientated I feel something very light land on my outstretched hands.

I look at what I am holding, and to my surprise I see a very long and narrow feather of gold, which is almost transparent. Absolutely amazed at what my eyes behold, I sit down on a nearby rock to support me, as I am feeling a little fragile.

As I look down, ready to bury my face in my hands, I notice my clothes are different. I am wearing a knee length dress with long sleeves that go wider from my wrists. They almost cover my hands. It is a light, natural green colour and made of a lightweight material, but not transparent.

As I am still looking down, a piece of paper catches my eye. I bend down and pick it up. When I stand back up, I look at it more closely. It looks like a shopping list of ingredients of different plant life, like camomile, lavender and various different flower petals and their nectar.

I hear a movement, not far from where I am. I turn around and someone is standing in front of me. It is a woman, with short brown hair, hazel eyes, fair skin and wings of gold – like that of the feather I found. She is pretty but looks serious – actually she looks annoyed. I am standing here not knowing what to do.

She moves towards me and says, very crossly, "Have you any idea what you have done?" I look at her, feeling confused at her accusation, I don't understand. I am quiet. She moves closer to me, more aggressive than before, grabs me by my arms and shakes me, saying, "Well? You have consumed of this place, which means you may never go back to where you come from. You don't belong here."

I reply, "Is it your place to say these words to me? You say I have consumed of this place, what does that mean? And how would you know?"

Just as she is about to reply, we both hear fluttering close by. A man appears behind her, hovering. He says, "Enough talk, what is done is done." He turns to me and continues, "This place is now your home. Come, let me show you around."

Naomi Wilson

Subway : Melanie Macdonald

Black

My bull's name is Black. This bull is for my prestige, Black means rich.

I am rich enough to marry ten wives.

Black is a symbol of one family.

Black is always sang in our traditional dances.

It is also sang when I'm herding the cattle.

During dry seasons, my bull Black is being admired by my girlfriends. They always make sure they see Black before I take the cattle to eat.

When I come back from the field, they bring water and additional grass for Black.

Therefore, I am mostly popular in my village.

Daniel Yupet

The Box [6]

A box is square with nothing in it

A box can be filled if you want it

A box is brown and plain

A box cannot see my pain

A box looks dull, but not when the box is full

A box can be what you want it to be

But a box is still nothing to me.

Kaz

Bob the dog : Robert Sutton

Drinking Part 2

I wake up in the morning, the phone rings. I wonder who
that is – is it Lee, is it Colette? No, it's Angela.
"Rob, have you got a spiff?" I say, no, but then I go and
buy some. And as I get mellowed I say I'm giving up
smoking the wacky after this bit, but I go back on my word.

I am weak when it comes to temptation, I need to take care
of myself more – this wacky doesn't help. Gran says,
"What's that funny smell?" and I say it's deodorant.

Going to a party tonight. I'll be all right if I only have two
drinks.

Two drinks? No way, you're more likely to say. I'll have it
my way and I'll drink all day. Where's my dog, Bob?

Robert Sutton

Myrtle's Story

I was born in Jamaica
In a district called Clarendon.
When I was seventeen, I went to Kingston
Had three children and came to England
It was 1961

One child came with me
One is now in Canada
One is still in Jamaica
And then I had another two children in England
A girl and a boy

I'm retired now
I've done machining over the years
I lived in Bolton for six months
Then I moved to Manchester, England
I worked all my life

I worked as a machinist.
I worked on pillowcases,
For an American firm in Oldham
I worked on coats for firms all over England
Working in Manchester

I have nine grandchildren now
Three in Canada, I visit them occasionally,
They live in Ontario
Three in Jamaica and three in England
I visit them all, when I can.

Aunty Myrtle
Edited by Alkimu

Boat

Roll, roll, roll your boat gently by the stream
Merrily, merrily, merrily, merrily, life is but a dream

A boat is a carving used by people in the water (river) to move from one place to another. On the boat, you can sit there to catch fishes, transportation of things from one place to another, sitting in a boat with families and loved ones, very interesting for sightseeing. I desire to roll a boat - just me, my husband and my son.

Uche

Be Strong

Big and wide
Void and Dark
Creatures moving round and round
Continents to Continents
Wandering and becoming wandersome
Lonely and lost
Thirst fail
Hunger linger
Life's lost
Inclusion and exclusion
Yet a voice in the wilderness
...BE STRONG

Olayinka Arowosegbe

Hurdles

I open the box
And what do I
Find?
Another box
A box of another
Kind

Within the box
Layer upon layer
There are boxes
Of all different
Types

It's like in life
As soon as I have
Overcome one hurdle
I come against
Another

I'm standing there
Thinking 'Oh bother!'

Then I tell myself, 'You
Can do it girl!'
I then trip, break into
A skip, grab the lamppost
And I do a twirl

As I come to a halt
A friend passing by
Says, 'Did you enjoy
Your journey?'

Naomi Wilson

Psalm 27

We lived in the district and my parents were too strict
I was different from the others
When the sun was hot – ninety degrees
I came from church
While everyone else would study outside
I was made to stay in
They were all talking against me
So I decided to join another church
We children had to sit at the back
While the adults did communion
Me want to find out what it about
So with fourteen other girls from the district
I started lessons – six months before baptism.
It was 1947
When I got baptised and I sang
I have decided to follow Jesus
No turning back
And until now I have never turned back
Not when my children scatter
And do their own things
Not when I came to England
I'm going on just the same
Nothing change me
I came with my Bible and Two hymns
Psalm 27
Take the name of Jesus with you
Guide me oh thou great Jehovah

Mrs Burke
Edited by Alkimu

Christmas

Christmas is over-rated
Blown way out of proportion
Wrapped up in 'a time for giving'
Distributed with good cheer and wishes
When really it's just so commercial
A time of greed and exploitation
'You need this' and 'You need that'
When really, you managed the whole year
I'm sure you'll survive without it
If Santa doesn't deliver this year

Sophie Davies

The dark room

I walk into a dark room, after the long corridor that we have just come from. The walls are cold and disturbed. I take a breath of the cold, damp air and look around - I feel scared. There is a presence in the room that I can feel, but I can't see, hear or smell.

The hairs on my neck start to rise and I can feel someone looking into my eyes. I know they're there, but they're not showing themselves; my fear spreads and starts growing and then I see a girl in the corner of the dark, grim room. She stands laughing, like I've just done something funny, but I haven't. She walks closer, puts her hand on my shoulder, and that's the last thing I remember.

Now I'm sat in a corner of another dark room, and I hear someone coming. A girl walks through the door, and looks around. Looking scared, I start laughing and walk over to her and touch her on the shoulder. She falls to the floor, she doesn't breathe no more.

Then I realise what has happened. That was me. When I was here, when I walked in that room, that girl looked at me, me, my death replayed like it was on TV, and this replay will never stop, the day I walked in and then I dropped.

Kaz

I am

I am who I am!
I don't care what
You think
Even if I do wear
Pink
I refuse to feel
Blue
Because of you!

Naomi Wilson

I want

I want what's best
For me
If it means climbing
The tree of Calvary
To shout 'I don't
care!'
Even though you stare,
So what, you can
See we make a good
Pair

Bobby Dog

I am stood here with Bobby Dog
And he's got big froggy eyes
I say – Bob
He takes no notice of me
Cos he's a big, fat alsation
He barks and likes to bite the postman
Not the women

For breakfast and every day
I wake up
He's the one barking for me
Because he likes a cup of tea with me

Robert Sutton

A box [7]

A box...
What is a box?
What does a box mean to you?
Me?
Yes
For me it means a present
It might have something inside
Oh, what could be in there?
I don't know
Maybe a necklace
Could be empty
It is square
Why does a box have to be a square?
Tell me what's inside
No
Guess
It makes me curious
I imagine things
What it is like inside
It is dark
Light
It is happy
Sad

Julmira Antonio

The Seamstress

My mother was a seamstress
And my father was a builder
There were eight of us children
Five girls and three boys
We were born in St Vincent

I married and when I was twenty-five
We went to Aruba, to the oil refinery
Forty two thousand they employed
From the Caribbean

My eight children were four girls
And four boys and all of them schooled
In the war my son repaired
Bombers until the company found
Automation

My husband died and I came
To England in 1961
What a journey on the Lady Nelson
To Barbados then New York
From New York to London
Train to Manchester

They told us the streets were paved with gold
During the war we all had money
Took from our wages, we were British you see
And it was for our war
Everyone had money taken from his or her wages
I didn't find golden streets

Living in Moss Side I worked at Pickerings
Wrapping papers in the cold factory
I moved towards the pipe that was warm
The charge hand moved me on
Whites only – I didn't like Pickerings
But I lived in a room with a nurse from
Barbados and sent £3.50 every month
To my mother and aunt to take care of my children

For nineteen years, six months and five days
I worked as a cook until my last boy left grammar
School and he was told to go home
No good jobs, he was fit for the factory
But not my boy, I sent him to college with
Two Pepsi's and money for food and travel

No handouts for my children.
I'd prefer to go naked than they take handouts
Today my youngest is 52 and since he was 18
He has worked at Dunlop's, in the office
My cooking paid off, he is married with
Three children, my grandchildren

Mrs Innis
Edited by Alkimu

Contact Details

Brian Chapman
Director **LIME**
St Mary's Hospital
Hathersage Road
Manchester
M13 OJH
Tel: 0161 256 4389
E-Mail: brian@limeart.org

Muli Amaye & Kim Wiltshire
ALKIMU
Ada House
77 Thompson Street
Manchester
M4 5FY
Tel: 0161 833 8818
Email: alkimu_alkimu@yahoo.co.uk

Cover Photography   Melanie Macdonald
Cover and Publication Design   Toshi Dog Design
Print   Nornir